Walter the Pigeon

Walter the Pigeon

James Birch

Illustrated by Raisa Veikkola

To all the pigeons in the world on this rocky road of Love

Preface

Thank you Alastair Brotchie for your continuous support and for making this happen, Hannah Watson and late Gigi Giannuzzi of Trolley Books for giving it a home, Marcus Campbell and Barry Miles for their help at the beginning of this project, and Liam Ryan for the Mount Pleasant photograph. Lastly, thank you Martine Grimal for the initial inspiration (who must be on her 8th husband by now...).

Introduction

I found this manuscript in the bottom of a drawer when I was looking for something completely different. I wrote this simple and sad love story at the end of my teenage years and it had been lost and forgotten, collecting dust for decades. I had made some illustrations for it at the time but they are long gone. Luckily I met Raisa Veikkola over a falafel lunch who agreed to illustrate this story. I am glad for it to finally see the light of day.

Walter the Pigeon

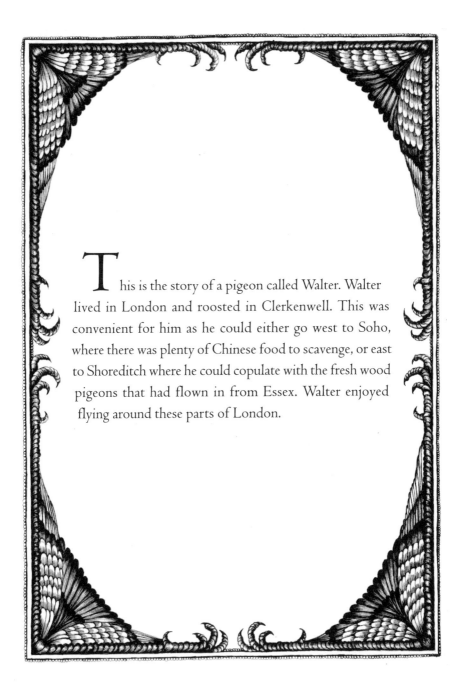

This is the story of a pigeon called Walter. Walter lived in London and roosted in Clerkenwell. This was convenient for him as he could either go west to Soho, where there was plenty of Chinese food to scavenge, or east to Shoreditch where he could copulate with the fresh wood pigeons that had flown in from Essex. Walter enjoyed flying around these parts of London.

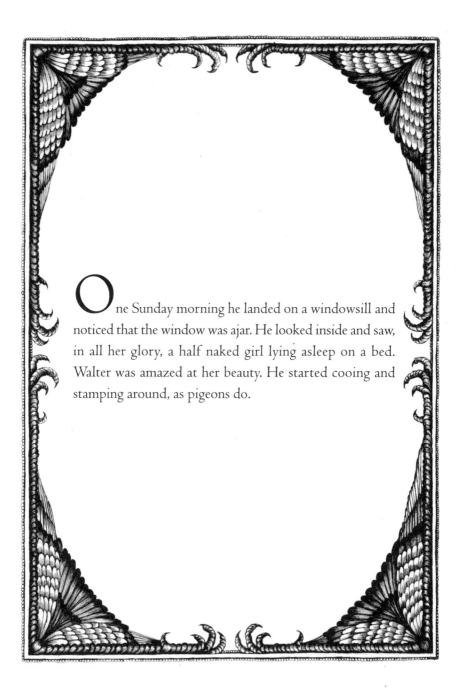

One Sunday morning he landed on a windowsill and noticed that the window was ajar. He looked inside and saw, in all her glory, a half naked girl lying asleep on a bed. Walter was amazed at her beauty. He started cooing and stamping around, as pigeons do.

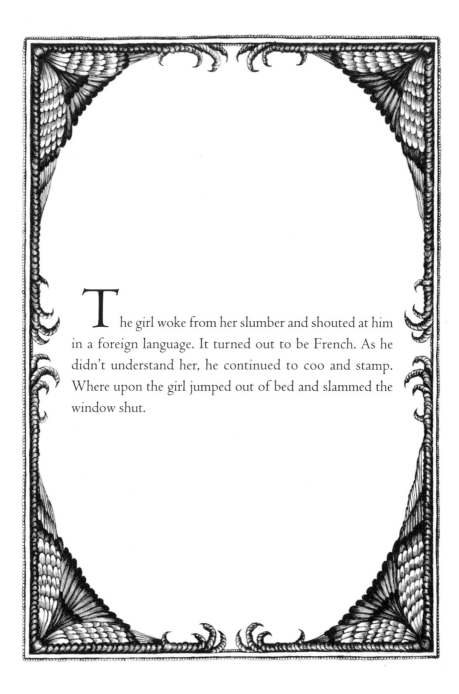

The girl woke from her slumber and shouted at him in a foreign language. It turned out to be French. As he didn't understand her, he continued to coo and stamp. Where upon the girl jumped out of bed and slammed the window shut.

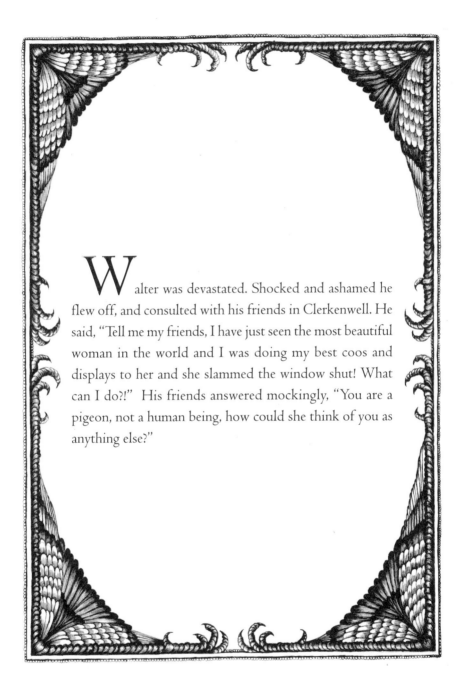

Walter was devastated. Shocked and ashamed he flew off, and consulted with his friends in Clerkenwell. He said, "Tell me my friends, I have just seen the most beautiful woman in the world and I was doing my best coos and displays to her and she slammed the window shut! What can I do?!" His friends answered mockingly, "You are a pigeon, not a human being, how could she think of you as anything else?"

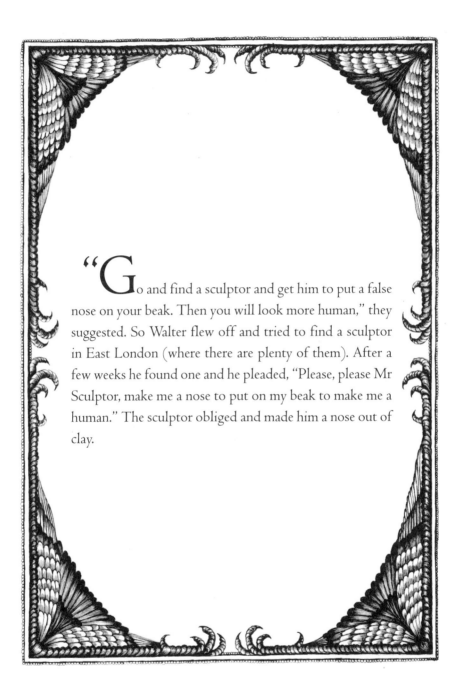

"Go and find a sculptor and get him to put a false nose on your beak. Then you will look more human," they suggested. So Walter flew off and tried to find a sculptor in East London (where there are plenty of them). After a few weeks he found one and he pleaded, "Please, please Mr Sculptor, make me a nose to put on my beak to make me a human." The sculptor obliged and made him a nose out of clay.

With a new nose on his beak, he felt proud and paraded his new attire to his friends. They laughed at him, but he didn't mind because he now knew that he could go back to the windowsill of the beautiful girl and capture her heart.

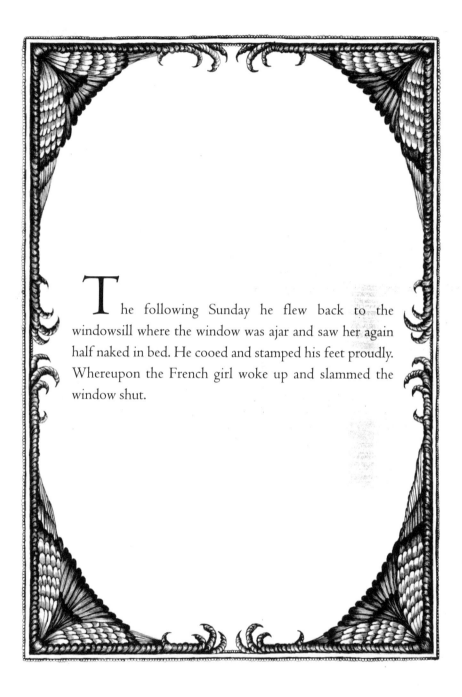

The following Sunday he flew back to the windowsill where the window was ajar and saw her again half naked in bed. He cooed and stamped his feet proudly. Whereupon the French girl woke up and slammed the window shut.

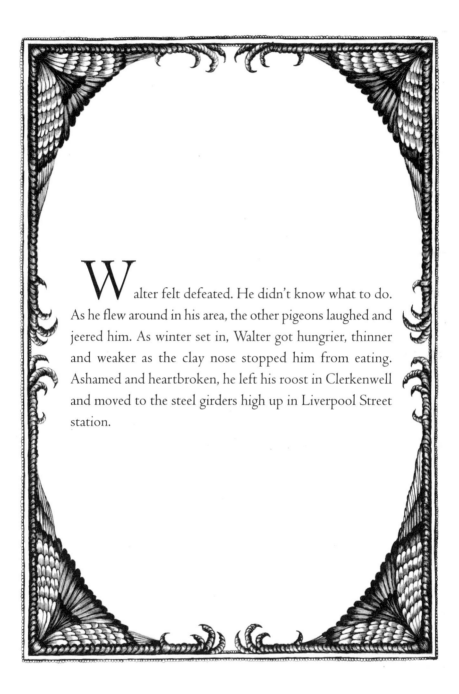

Walter felt defeated. He didn't know what to do. As he flew around in his area, the other pigeons laughed and jeered him. As winter set in, Walter got hungrier, thinner and weaker as the clay nose stopped him from eating. Ashamed and heartbroken, he left his roost in Clerkenwell and moved to the steel girders high up in Liverpool Street station.

One Sunday morning, as he was perched trembling with cold and hunger, he looked down and saw the French girl walking arm in arm with a man.

With the weight of the nose and his heart broken, he fell from the rafters and landed two feet in front of the couple, dead.

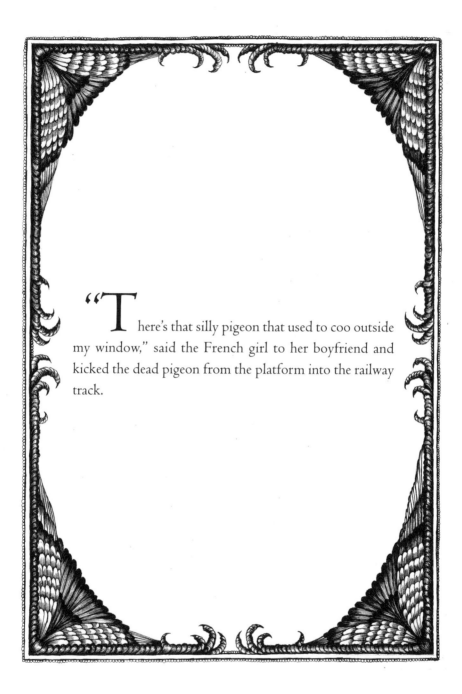

"There's that silly pigeon that used to coo outside my window," said the French girl to her boyfriend and kicked the dead pigeon from the platform into the railway track.

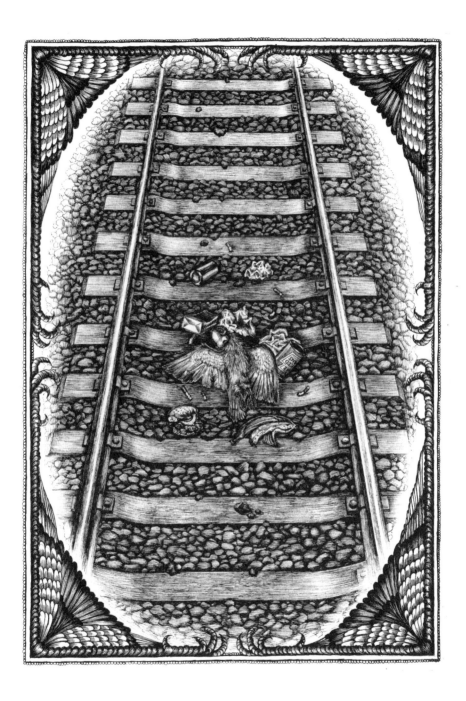

The moral of the story is —

don't have a nose job.